rez dogs

More by Joseph Bruchac

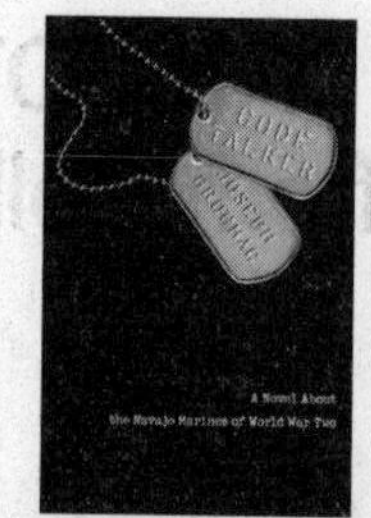

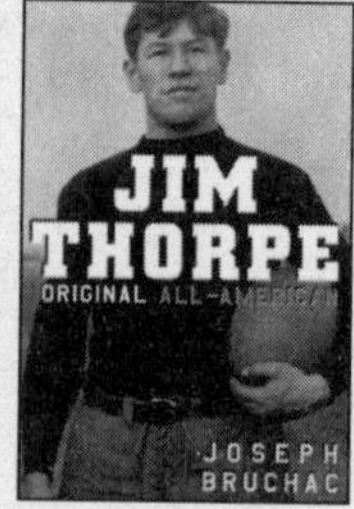

JOSEPH BRUCHAC

Dial Books
for Young Readers

DIAL BOOKS FOR YOUNG READERS
An imprint of Penguin Random House LLC, New York

First published in the United States of America by Dial Books for Young Readers, 2021
First paperback edition published 2022

Visit us online at penguinrandomhouse.com.

THE LIBRARY OF CONGRESS HAS CATALOGED THE HARDCOVER EDITION AS FOLLOWS:
Library of Congress Cataloging-in-Publication Data
Names: Bruchac, Joseph, date, author.
Title: Rez dogs / Joseph Bruchac.
Description: New York : Dial Books for Young Readers, 2021. | Audience: Ages 8–12 | Audience: Grades 4–6 | Summary: "Twelve-year-old Malian lives with her grandparents on a Wabanaki reservation during the COVID-19 pandemic"— Provided by publisher.
Identifiers: LCCN 2021015241 (print) | LCCN 2021015242 (ebook) | ISBN 9780593326213 (hardcover) | ISBN 9780593326237 (ebook)
Subjects: CYAC: Novels in verse. | Abenaki Indians—Fiction. | COVID-19 (Disease)—Fiction. | Quarantine—Fiction. | Grandparents—Fiction. | Indians of North America—Northeastern States—Fiction.
Classification: LCC PZ7.B82816 Rez 2021 (print) | LCC PZ7.B82816 (ebook) | DDC [Fic]—dc23
LC record available at https://lccn.loc.gov/2021015241
LC ebook record available at https://lccn.loc.gov/2021015242
Printed in the United States of America

ISBN 9780593326220

5th Printing

LSCH

Design by Mina Chung
Text set in Clearface ITC Pro

For all of those in our communities
who worked with such courage
to support each other

chapter one

malsum

When Malian woke up
and looked out her window,
the dog was there.
Just as she had
dreamed it would be.

It was lying on the driveway
halfway between
their small house and the road.

It wasn't sleeping,
its head was up,
its ears erect,
its paws in front of it

as if on guard.
As Malian watched,
the dog turned its head
to look right at her,
as if it knew her,
as if it had known her
for a long, long time.

“Malsum,” she said.
“Kwai, kwai, nidoba.”
Hello, hello, my friend.

The big dog nodded
and then turned back
to continue watching the road.

Malsum. That was
the old name for a wolf.
It was a good one for that dog.
It was as big as a wolf.
It looked like the videos
of wolves she’d watched

on her phone.
The only things different
about it were the white spots
over each of its eyes.

"Four-eyed dog,"
a soft voice said
from back over her shoulder.

It was Grandma Frances.
Malian had not
heard her come up behind.
She was used to that.
Both her grandparents
could walk so softly
that she never knew
they were there
until they spoke.

Grandma Frances
would tease her about it.
"Be careful, granddaughter,

you don't want
to let no Indian
sneak up on you."
Grandma Frances
put her hand
on Malian's shoulder.
"Looks to me
like he thinks
he belongs here," she said.
Then she chuckled.
"Or maybe like
he thinks he
owns this place."

"Would that be okay?"
Malian said.

Grandma Frances
chuckled again.
"It seems to me
it's not up to us.
When a dog like
that just appears

and chooses you,
it's not your decision."

"Can I go outside and see
what he does?" Malian said.

"Let's ask your grampa.
Roy, get in here."

But Grampa Roy
was already there.
"I've been listening
to every word.
Seems to me
if you step outside
and then move real slow
whilst you watch what he does
you'll be okay.
But just in case,
I'll be right behind you."

Malian shook her head.
"Remember what they said?

You and Grandma
should not go outside.
It's too dangerous—
you might get that virus.
That's why I can't
go home to Mom and Dad."

"And we're goldarn lucky
you're here with us,"
Grampa Roy said.
"That old saying about
how we don't know
what we'd do without you
sure makes sense these days.
So I'll stay inside—
but you stay in, too.
Just open the door
and we'll see what he does."

Malian cracked open the door.
The dog stood up
and turned her way.

He opened his mouth,
let his tongue hang out
in what she knew
had to be a smile.

She held out her wrist.
"Malsum!" she called,
her voice soft but sure.

The big dog walked over
and sniffed her hand.

"Malsum," she said again,
dropping down to one knee
as she placed her hand
on his broad head.

The dog looked at her,
straight into her eyes.
As he held her gaze
it seemed to Malian
that she could see

intelligence and
even a hint of humor
and a kind of certainty.

Malsum nodded his head
as if to say, *Yes*
that can be my name.
I am here for you.
Then he licked her fingers
before turning around
and going back,
heavy muscles rippling
beneath his skin,
to drop himself down
where he had been.

"Guess he is
guarding us, for sure,"
Grampa Roy said.
"Looks like you got
a new friend."

chapter two

rez dogs

Malsum was lying
on his back, his tongue
hanging out
as Malian rubbed his stomach.

She was thinking
about how cool
it was that their names
sort of sounded the same.
Even though
his meant "wolf"
and hers was just
the way her old
Penacook people,
who didn't use the

sound of *l*,
pronounced "Mary Ann."

"Yup," Grampa Roy said,
nodding his head,
"there's just no doubt
that he's chosen you."

He tapped his long
index finger on his chin,
a gesture her grandfather
often made just before
he was to tell a story.

"The dogs on any reservation,
they have their own lives.
They have their own tribes,
and when we would travel,
like when in the spring
we used to go and live
by the falls where the fish
were running,

lots of times the dogs
would not go with us.
They'd stay in the village
and take care of themselves."

He chuckled. "You know,
my grampa Red Hawk
told me how one time
when they'd gone
to the falls, he realized
that he'd left his best
knife behind, and so
he went back to get it.
He also wondered
just what the dogs
were doing with all
the people gone.
So he snuck up
to the edge of the village.
My grampa always
could move real quiet,
and he stayed downwind

so they couldn't smell him.
So I guess none of those
dogs knew he was there
when he peeked out
from behind a tree.
And what he saw
was the darnedest thing.
Those dogs were acting
just like people.
They'd put on clothes
we left behind
and some of them
were walking around
on their hind legs.
Some were sitting
around the fire
and drinking soup
from wooden cups
that they dipped into
a pot that they had cooking.
One of them was even
smoking a pipe.
Grampa Red Hawk

figured the best thing
he could do was just
leave those dogs be.
So he didn't bother
to look for his knife.
He just made his way
back to the falls.

"What it showed him
was that the dogs
could do just fine
on their own without us.
We humans were lucky
they chose to live with us.
Or maybe it was
the other way around—
that we were the ones who chose
to live with them."

The big dog had sat up
when Grampa Roy
started to tell that story.
As soon as it was done,

he stood, shook himself,
and then walked over
to Grampa Roy
to put one paw in his lap
and look into his face.

"Did I get it right?"
Grampa Roy said.
Malsum nodded and then
went back to lie down
in front of Malian.

Grampa Roy smiled.
"Yup, our rez dogs
are not like them
you see in the cities.
You'll never see
our good friend here
being walked around
on some fancy leash."

Malian smiled back
at her grandfather.

She always loved it
when he told her stories.
She also smiled
because she knew
how true it was about the dogs
on the rez being different
from those in the cities.

She'd noticed that
when she was little
and made her very first trip
to Boston with her parents
for her father's interview
with that big law firm.

She was only five,
but she had to ask,
"Why are all those dogs
tied to people like that?
Don't they have any
lives of their own?
How come they're not
just allowed to run free?"

Her dad went down on one knee,
put his hands on her shoulders.
"It's just kind of the way
not only the dogs
but the people have to live
in the city where they're
all so close together.
If they're not controlled,
they might get hurt
or maybe even hurt each other."

That was when her mom
smiled down at her dad
and said, "Well now, Thomas,
it seems to me you could say
that we are rez dogs too."

"Woof," Malian said.
"Woof, woof, woof!"

Then all three of them
started barking
and laughing together,

no one else walking by
understanding
why they were barking,
maybe not even knowing
the three of them were
Indians—Dad in his suit,
Mom in her best jeans,
and Malian in her new
Catholic school uniform,
three rez dogs in the city.
That was how she
saw them back then
and saw herself still.

chapter three

mail delivery

Malsum sensed
the mailman first
as Malian sat with the big dog
on the crooked
old wooden steps.
Her dad had planned
to fix those steps
after he and her mother
got back from the city.
But that was before
they had to shelter

in place in the city
and Malian's weekend visit
to her grandparents
on the rez
got stretched out
way, way longer.

A deep growl started
in Malsum's throat,
then he stood up
and walked stiff-legged
to stand at the end
of the walk
by the mailbox
thirty feet from their front door.

He didn't move
as the truck pulled up
and a red-haired man
in a uniform
started to get out.
But he stopped

as Malsum's
growl got louder.
"Call off your dog,"
the man yelled,
then started coughing.

Malian stayed where she was,
and, ahead of her now,
so did Malsum.

The mailman wiped
his nose on his sleeve,
then held up a box.
"I got a package
you need to sign for."

"Thank you, mister,"
Malian called to him,
"but whatever it is,
I don't think I need it.
I also think that maybe
what you need now
is to go see a doctor."

The mailman started
coughing again.
When it stopped, he nodded.
"Kid, you might be right."
Then he smiled,
held up his hand.
He took a pen
from his shirt pocket
and scribbled something
on the piece of paper
stuck to the top of the box.

"Guess what," he said.
"It looks to me like you
already signed for this."
He balanced the package
on top of the mailbox.
"I'll go by the clinic today."
He coughed as he slid
back behind the wheel.

"You and Killer there
take good care

of Roy and Martha Frances.
Tell 'em Al said hi."

Malian waited on the steps
until the truck was out of sight
and the big dog came
back to her side.
Then she put on
the vinyl gloves
from the box inside the door,
pulled out some tissues
from the baby wipe dispenser
before getting the package.

It had been sent
by her parents, of course.
She wiped it down
on every side
before opening it.

BEARS ALWAYS HAVE
TO HAVE
THEIR SWEETS,

read the note
her mom had written.
SO THESE ARE FOR
YOUR GRANDPARENTS
AND YOU, OUR SWEET, SWEET GIRL.

Inside were eight packages
of the cookies that she
and her grandparents loved.

Her father's words
written on the back
of her mother's note
were in smaller print,
but they were even sweeter.

Malian, you are the best
daughter and granddaughter
in the whole wide world.
We miss you so much,
but we're glad you're there.
That's the way our Creator
meant it to be, that one day

young people might know
the blessing of being able
to take care of those
who cared for them
when they were young.
Give them a hug from both of us.
We'll all be together soon.

Malsum looked up
quizzically, as if
asking why he
had been left out.

Malian knelt and
put her arms
around Malsum's neck.
"Don't feel bad, boy.
I haven't told them
about you yet."

She stood up and took
her iPhone out.
"Look at me," she said,

"smile for the camera."
The big dog looked up,
then opened his mouth
in a grin so wide,
it made Malian laugh.

"All right," she said
as she pressed SEND.
"My mom and dad
are going to be glad
that we have
such a great new friend."

chapter four

three muskrateers

Her phone was ringing.
She picked it up
and looked at the time.
It was midnight.
Who would be calling her at midnight?
Her daily call from her parents
had taken place just after dinner.
Her grandparents had been in bed
for two hours already.

"Hello?" she said.
"Help!" replied the voice
on the other end.
"Who is this?"
"It's us," said a

sort of familiar voice.
"It's us, the Three Muskrateers."

It was Darrell Muskwas.
Of course, Malian thought.
Who else would be
calling up this late?
He and his two best buddies,
the Glossian twins,
Abel and Mark, started
calling themselves that
a couple of years ago.

Darrell's last name
in Wabanaki meant "muskrat."
Unlike Malian, the three of them
had never read Alexander Dumas,
but they'd loved the movie.

The three of them
were not bad kids.
But if there was
any trouble

you could get into
around the rez,
they would be
knee-deep in it
before you could
say Tabat! Stop!

Malian had
known those guys
since all four of them
were real little.
Whenever she spent time
with her grandparents,
usually during
the summer vacation,
those three guys were who
she almost always
ended up
hanging out with.

Even though she'd been
living off rez
since kindergarten,

they'd pretty much
accepted her—
even though Darrell
had started
the three of them
calling her Macintosh.

Macintosh, the apple
and not the computer.
It was a play on
the slang word *Apple,*
a name for someone
who looks Indian
but acts more
like a white person—
red on the outside
and white within.
An insult to say
to somebody Native.

But they said it
good-naturedly,
and Malian

was never one
to let words hurt her,
especially since
she knew
real well
who she was.

"Why are you calling me
at midnight?" she asked.

"Because we need help,"
Darrell pleaded.

"What kind of help
do you need?"

Darrell's voice
was strained.

"We need you now!
Right now! To keep
your dog from eating us.

We're way up
in the old ash tree
across the road.
And your big dog
is here snarling
at the base of the tree,
jumping up at us
and growling
like a werewolf!"

Malian barely managed
to keep herself
from laughing out loud.

"What did you do
to make him chase you?"

There was a long silence
from the other end.
Then Darrell said,
"The three of us
sneaked out of our houses.

We came over
to your place
just to see
if maybe you'd like
to come out with us.
You know,
just do something.
It's so boring at home."

Malian had to agree
that it sure was
boring at times.
She wished she could
hang out with friends;
if not the kids
she'd gotten to know
in her school,
then her Penacook buddies,
like the Muskrateers.
Would it really hurt
to just spend

a little time
out of the house
with them?

Then she shook her head.
The way things were,
she had to be
responsible—
she couldn't
think first about fun
like a little kid.

"Right now?"
Malian said,
putting on her
grown-up voice.
"At night
in the middle
of a pandemic?"

"Aw," Darrell said,

"come on, Malian.
Everyone knows
what we've heard
on the news.
Kids don't get
this disease,
so isn't it crazy
for us to stay
all cooped up
like chickens.
Anyhow, we
sneaked up real good
and were just about
to throw some little
stones at your window
to wake you up,
when we heard
this deep growl!
Then your big dog
came charging out
and us three,
we barely made it

to this tree."
This time it was even harder
for Malian not to laugh,
but she didn't.

"Okay," she said,
her voice calm.
"I will go call him,
but you have to
promise me something."

"Whatever you ask,
we'll do it,"
Darrell said.

"Okay," she said.
"Now, first of all,
maybe us kids
don't get COVID-19
as bad as adults do,
but we can give it
to our elders.

You three guys all
have grandparents at home.
So you should be
ashamed of yourselves."

There was an even
longer silence.

Then Darrell said,
in a quieter voice,
"You got a point."

"You bet I do.
Now if you really
agree with me
I'm going
to whistle and call
our dog back to me
and you three
are going
to climb down
from that tree

and go straight home.
All right?"

There was a long pause
and she could hear
a muffled sound like grumbling
from the Muskrateers,
probably muffled
because Darrell
had his hand
over his phone.

"Oh-kay," Darrell
finally sighed
in a resigned voice.
"We guess you're right."

Malian whistled.
Malsum stood,
shook himself,
took one last look
up the tree,

then trotted
to her side.

Trying not
to laugh,
Malian watched
as the boys
climbed down,
then called to them:

"Good night!"

chapter five

frybread

Malian put her
iPad aside, sighed,
and leaned against
the porch railing.
Malsum, who
was sitting by her feet,
turned his head
and looked at her,
as if to ask
if she needed help.

Malian looked at him
and shook her head.
"It's okay, boy.
There's nothing
you can do to help"
—she held up her iPad—
"with this."

She tapped the icon again.
Nothing!

It was so frustrating
trying to do
anything online
here on the rez.
Even here outside
she sometimes couldn't
get enough bars
on her personal hotspot
to connect.

Ms. Mendelson, her teacher,
had been understanding.
"Just connect when you can
and if you miss class,
don't worry because
I'll always e-mail you
the assignments so
you can keep up."

That was good,
but still, Malian didn't like
to always have to
be playing catch-up.
Back in Boston,
she was always
one of the first
to hand in
her assignments.
Her dad had taught her
that was one way
to avoid being seen
by narrow-minded people
as a "lazy Indian."

She sighed again,
louder this time.

Malsum, who'd
been sitting by her side,
looked up at her,

then carefully placed
one of his big paws
in her lap.

Malian patted him
on the head.
His friendship helped,
but it simply couldn't
solve everything.

She sometimes
felt so cut off,
it was like she was
floating in midair.

Unlike the other kids
here on the rez,
like the Muskrateers,
Malian wasn't used
to going to a school
that was barely in
the twenty-first century

without any Wi-Fi
and spotty Internet.

She had heard
how off-rez kids
like her Boston classmates
with all their
high-speed connections
were having trouble
doing things at home,
especially with all the strain
of being with family
all day, every day.

She loved her grandparents,
but kind of envied
those kids stuck
with moms and dads.
She really missed
her mother and father
so much that at times
it seemed

as if her heart
was going to break.

Malsum made
a soft greeting sound.
Ha-woof, ha-woof!
Malian turned
her head to look.
Her grandmother
stood there
in the doorway,
a plate of warm frybread
and a jar of honey
in her hands.

"Like some of this, darling?
Mitsi da? Want to eat?"

"Onh-honh!"
Malian said,
at the very same time
as Malsum made
the small growling sound

he always made
whenever he was
offered food.

Malian had to smile
as she looked at him.
"Malsum," she said,
"you're a real Indian dog."

She smiled for herself, too.
She was always ready
to eat frybread,
and her grandmother's
was really, really good.

"Ktsi wliwini, Nokomis.
Thanks so much, Grandma."

They each broke off
a small piece
of the warm brown bread
and placed it
under the cedar tree

to share it with
the Manogies,
the little people
who are the guardians
of the natural world.
Malsum sat
and watched
as they did that.
Somehow the big dog
always seemed to know
food offered like that
was not for him
and he never
tried to take it.
But it was always
gone the next morning.
Her grandmother
sat on the steps
beside her.

"Your father loves
my frybread too,"
Grandma Frances said

as she offered
a small piece
of the bread
to Malsum,
who gently took it
from her.

"You know,"
she continued,
"I usually win
the competition
at our festival
for the best frybread
just about every year."
Malian nodded,
not able to talk
because her mouth
was already full.

As she ate,
her grandmother
started to sing
a thank-you song—

its words so old,
there was no way
to say them in English,
though Malian
could understand
what they meant.

Malian thought
about frybread.
How Native people
all over the continent
made it and everyone
did it their own way.

It was made
of white flour
and lard and sugar—
commodity goods,
the meager rations
the United States
government provided

to honor the treaties
her people had been
forced to sign
in which
they gave up
most of their land.
The cheapest and
the worst kind of stuff
in place of the old-time
nutritious foods.

Yet Indian people
had made it their own.
Just like
so many other things
brought by
the Europeans.

"I remember,"
her grandmother said,
"the first time your mother

had my frybread.
She said it was like
a taste of heaven.

"You know, her being
taken away like that
when she was so little,
she never grew up
eating frybread."

Malian nodded.
Her mom had told her
the story more than once.
How when she was little
social services
people took her
away from her parents—
saying they were unfit.

They were not bad parents,
but they were just poor,
being Indian and all.
That sort of thing happened

to so many Native kids—
all the way
up into the '90s.
Whenever people saw
social services coming,
they would try to hide
their kids away to keep
them from being taken.

The ironic thing,
Malian thought,
about her mom being
taken away,
is that it was
almost the same
as what happened
to her grandparents.

When they were little
the Indian School
Attendance Officers
would come
and drag them away.

Whenever her grandmother
talked about that,
she actually quoted
a famous white man—
an American philosopher
named Henry David Thoreau
who lived about
two hundred years ago.

Her grandmother
was always reading
and had three shelves
full of books on her wall.
So it wasn't surprising
that she knew
about Thoreau.

"It was Mr. Thoreau,"
her grandmother said,
"who wrote that if
you see someone coming
to your house
with the express purpose

of doing good for you,
leave quickly
by the back door."
It was from
her grandmother
that Malian also learned
how Mr. Thoreau loved
the New England Indians.

"So much that
he'd planned
to write a big book
all about us
but he died
at a real young age."

Her grandmother
shook her head.
"It just might be
the happiest times
of his life
were when he was
up in the Maine woods

being guided by Joe Polis,
that same Penobscot
Indian guide
who was your
great-great-great-
grandfather."

Her grandmother
dribbled honey onto
another piece of frybread
for Malian,
then gave more
of the still warm bread
to Malsum, who,
though drooling,
was waiting patiently.

"After your mother got
snatched up by those
social workers,
she ended in foster care."

Malian nodded
as she bit into
her second piece
of frybread.
Her mother had told her
that foster care
was like purgatory,
someplace
with no address
and stuck
in between
heaven and hell.

"That was when that
nice white family
the Wintons came
and adopted her.
But as soon as she
was old enough,
and off in college,
she began to search

for her own family
and found they came
from our reservation,
though all of them
by then had walked on.
Those Wintons,
George and Ethel,
they were good people.
I wish you could
have met them,
but they were already
in their fifties
when they took
in your mom
and a year before
you were born,
when your mom
was twenty-one,
they both passed on.

"When your mom
found out where

she came from,
those Wintons decided
the right thing to do
was to bring her here
for a visit.

"The very next summer
they rented
a summer home
near Penacook
and came up here.
She was just nineteen
and that July
was the one when
she met your father
at our annual
Penacook festival."

Malian smiled
as she remembered
how her mother laughed
when she spoke about that.

"Talk about an apple,"
her mother said.
"I was both the reddest
and the whitest one
in the entire barrel.
Your dad said I looked
like Indian Miss America,
but talked like a Valley girl.
Good thing I've always
been a quick learner."

Malian thought about that.
Even though she
was not being raised
on the reservation,
both her dad and her mom
were doing their best
to keep her connected
to who she really was.
That was why whenever
she came back
to the reservation
she felt at home.

And that was why
when the Three Muskrateers
called her Macintosh
it would just
roll off her,
like rain falling
on a duck's back.
"Want another piece
of frybread, darling?"
her grandmother asked.
"And maybe one
for Malsum, too?"

"You bet," Malian said,
holding out her hand
as the big dog growled
his agreement.

chapter six

our best best friend

Malian sat
on the front porch steps.
It had become
her usual spot.
She could see
across the yard
and onto the street
that opened up
into a wide circle
since it was
a dead-end road.

The only other
house in sight
was a hundred yards away.

Every now and then
the people in that house—
the Sabattis family—
would come out,
wave to her.
And she would wave back.

Malsum, as always,
sat next to her.
He had leaned
his wide head over
into her lap
and she was petting him.
He was such
a muscular dog.
His chest was broad,
his legs as strong
as those of a husky,
the sort of dog
she'd seen pulling sleds
as she watched a film
about that big race

that took place
up in Alaska every year.
She had heard that
many of those dogs
had a lot of wolf in them.
She smiled
at the thought of that.
You could say
that Malsum was a wolf
who had a lot
of dog in him.
He was licking her wrist
in a gentle way
that made her
feel like hugging him.
She'd never had
a dog of her own.
Where she and
her parents lived
in the city
it just wasn't possible.
Not unless

whatever dog they got
had to stay in all day
while she was at school
and her parents were at work.
And that was not fair.
A dog needs people
as much as people
need a dog.

Now, here on the rez,
was different—
a perfect place
to have a dog.
He could run free
through the small woods
behind the house,
even catch his own food.
Twice, he'd even
brought things he caught
back to them.
The first was a partridge
and the second

a snowshoe rabbit.
Her grandma
had cooked them both
into a stew—but only after
thanking the dog for his gift.

Her grandparents had
always had a dog.
Their last one, Willow,
had been with them
for fourteen years before
her spirit took the Sky Road.

They just hadn't yet
adopted another
before Malsum showed up
and adopted them.
They still had
the big bin out back
that Grampa Roy
kept filled with dry dog food,
so much that there

was more than enough
to take care of
their new friend
for a long time.

Her grandmother
came out and sat
down on the porch
next to them.
Malsum lifted his head
to lick her face.

"You be careful,"
Grandma Frances said,
"you're taking
off all my makeup.
I'm gonna look terrible
when the TV cameras
come to interview us."

Of course, there were
no TV folks coming.

It was just one
of Grandma's jokes.
She knew,
as did everyone else
on the rez,
that Indians were
pretty much the last people
anyone cared about
during this crisis.

Malian had read
in the weekly e-newsletter
from *Indian Country Today*
that Native people
were suffering some
of the biggest rates
of infections and deaths.
Especially on
the big Navajo reservation
way out west.
She'd helped her grandparents
make a donation
to a Navajo nation

relief fund with her phone.
Twenty dollars was all
they could afford,
but it meant a lot
to them to do it.
"Did you know,"
her grandfather had said,
"that way back
in the nineteenth century
when there was
that potato famine
over in Ireland,
some of our Indian people
pooled money together
and sent it to help them.
I hear that now
in the city of Dublin
they even put up
a statue to thank us."

That story
had almost
brought tears

to Malian's eyes.
Even thinking
about it now
she felt a lump
in her throat.
Her grandmother
stroked Malsum's back.
"I ever tell you,"
Grandma Frances said,
"how it came to be
that dogs always
walk beside us?
How it is they
are the only animals
on this old land
who've always lived
with us human beings?"

Malian shook her head.
"You haven't ever
told me that story."

And that was true,
she'd never heard
the story from her grandparents.

But her father
had told it to her
more than once.
It was usually
when they were talking
about how they were going
to move out of the city
once they had enough saved,
get a place in the country
where they could
have a dog of their own.

"Well," her grandmother said,
"I hear the way
it happened is this.
Long time ago
there were real big animals.

You've probably learned
about them in school.
Huge bears, giant elk,
all sorts like that,
even great big
hairy elephants
maybe ten thousand years ago."

Malian nodded.
In her biology class
they'd talked about
the megafauna
of the Pleistocene Era
here in North America.

"Well," her grandmother said,
stroking Malsum's back,
"what happened was this.
Gluskonba,
the one first shaped
like a human being,
was given power

by the Creator
to change things
and make them better
for the humans
who soon
would be here.

"One day,
Gluskonba,
he decided
to call the animals
together and ask
what they would do
when they saw
their first human.
The big ones
like the giant bear
and the giant moose
said that they
were going to destroy
every human being
that they saw.

Bear said it would
swallow them whole.
Moose said it would
spear all the humans
with its sharp horns,
then crush them.
So Gluskonba,
he took those big animals
and shaped them all down
so they're the size
they are today
and not so dangerous.
The most dangerous
one of all was Mikwe,
the red squirrel.
He was as big
as three elephants.
He said what he
was going to do
was tear every human
being into pieces.
So Gluskonba
shrunk that red squirrel

way down,
so small, it fit
in the palm of one hand.
Some animals did not
need to be
changed at all.
The rabbit said
it would just run away
when it saw a human
and the deer said
the very same thing.

"Finally,
all that was left
was just one animal
sitting there
and wagging its tail.
It was Dog, of course.

"'Are you going
to do something,'
Gluskonba asked,
'to hurt the humans

when you see them
for the first time?'
Dog shook his head.
'NO, NO, NO,' Dog said.
'I have just been waiting
for those people
to get here.
I want to hunt
and run by their side.
I want to live
in their homes with them,
watch over them
and guard their homes,
sleep by their fires,
play with their children
and be their best,
best friend.'

"Gluskonba nodded.
'That is how it will be.
You will always be
a friend to them,

a better friend than
some of them deserve.
From this day on
you will always live
with the humans
and you will be known
as Alemos—the one
who walks with us.'
And that is how
it is to this day.
Nialach?"

"Nialach,"
Malian repeated.
"So it is."

Malsum stood up
as if knowing
the story was ended.
He walked out
to the end of the walk
and then sat

looking down the road.
Grandma Frances
leaned over
and picked up
the plate
Malsum
had licked clean.

"Yup," she said,
nodding toward
the big dog,
"that's how it still is.
Living with us,
watching over us
to this very day."

chapter seven

beadwork

Malian lifted up her beadwork.
She studied it
in the afternoon light.
From across the kitchen table
her grandmother nodded.
"You are doing good,
granddaughter,
getting just about
as good as me."

Malian smiled.
No way was that true.
Her grandmother
was a champion beader.
The blue ribbons

hanging on her wall
from various powwows
where she won
first prize
were proof of that.

But, Malian thought,
I am getting pretty good.
The patterns
of ferns and flowers
within the piece
she'd been working on
were really nice.
She put her
beadwork down.

"I think I'm going
to go sit outside,"
she said.

Her grandmother nodded.
"Seeing as how
you've done

all your schoolwork
again for the day
and now you've gotten
so far on that bracelet,
seems to me
like you ought to go
and just rest your eyes.
Look up at the sky,
see how the wind
moves the clouds.
That's a better show
than most of what
we've been watching
on Netflix."

Malian nodded.
Her grandmother was right
about the sky being
so great to watch.

But she also knew
that her grandmother
enjoyed the movies

they watched together—
at least when
they could get reception.
They'd now binged
all the episodes
of the original
Star Trek series.
Both her grandparents
loved that show
and all the sequels
that followed.

There was even
one Star Trek series
where the captain
was Native American.
But that was not
their favorite one,
which was
The Next Generation.
As her grandfather
often said:

"Give me that
Captain Picard any day.
Now that's a future
I wouldn't mind living in."

Malian nodded
as she walked
past her grandfather,
sitting in his corner
working on a wooden bear.
He didn't look up,
just nodded.

Malian thought
about how lifelike
that bear was that
he'd almost finished.
Her grandfather's carving
made her remember
the story he'd told her
about four men
who tried to find

the hidden island
where Gluskonba went
after he'd finished doing
all he could for the people.

He'd left word
as he departed
that he'd grant one wish
to anyone who
could reach his island.

One of those four men
was a great woodcarver.
So great that if
he carved a turtle
and put it down
on the ground,
it would walk away.

Her grandfather
was just about
as good as that.

Before he retired
he had been
a master carpenter,
a skill he'd learned
while he was away
at the Indian school.

Between her grandfather's
retirement money
and what her grandmother
had put away
in her many years
as a primary teacher,
Malian's grandparents
had enough away
to take care of them
for the rest of their lives
"and then some,"
as her grandfather put it.

She opened the door
and stepped outside.

As she did so
she remembered something
that their PE teacher
back in Boston,
Mister Radgood,
was always saying.

Only boring people get bored.

I guess, Malian thought,
I'm a boring person.
Eight weeks of this
is way too much.

Even with the beadwork
and doing as much
of her homework
as she could each day
with their limited
Internet access,
she still felt like
she never had enough to do.

For the first four weeks,
she'd tried making lists
of things she had to do.
But one day when
she looked at her list
and saw she was writing down
Number 14. Trim my right big toenail
she realized list-making
was not for her.

Even though
it was dumb of them,
she could understand
why the Three Muskrateers
had been doing things
like what they did last week.
Which was
to pick the lock
on the gym door
of the high school
to go in at night
and play basketball.

No one actually
caught them at it,
but when she heard
her grandma talking
over the phone
to Maryagnes Polis—
who was still
the school's head cook—
about some kids
who broke into the gym,
Malian knew
who it had to be.

As she sat down,
Malsum came up
and sat on the steps
next to her.
The big dog never
went into the house,
even though
all three of them
had invited him in often.

He'd decided
his place was outside.

It was a warm
spring midafternoon.
The kind of day
that might make you
go in your garden
and plant your beans.
But, as Grampa Roy
had often told her,
rushing the season
was a foolish thing to do
seeing as how
the frost was sure
to come at least
once more before June.

Malsum pricked up his ears.
A low growl started
deep in his chest.
Then he stood up

and walked stiff-legged
to the end of the walk.
It was another minute
before Malian heard
what had alerted him.
A car was coming
up the road,
a white van
with letters on the side
that read

OFFICIAL GOVERNMENT

It stopped
and then
a blond woman
started to get out.
An officious look
was on her face,
a clipboard
in one hand
and a face mask
in the other.

She was not anyone
Malian knew,
but Malian knew
who she was.

Oh my,
Malian thought.
Social services.

Malsum took
four slow steps
toward the woman,
who stopped halfway
through putting on her mask.
His growling
got deeper
as he laid his ears
back flat across
his broad head
and took another step.

The woman
pulled her foot

back into the van,
slammed the door,
and rolled down the window.

"Call off your dog,"
the blond woman shouted.

"Not my dog,"
Malian called back to her,
cupping her hands
around her mouth.
"He belongs to himself."

The woman
looked puzzled
for a moment.
Then she seemed
to collect herself.

"I need to speak
to your grandparents,"
she said, not shouting now
but more controlled,

in a very stern voice.
"It came to our attention
you have been staying here.
We need to make sure
that this is a fit
environment for you
to be in."

Malian stood up
and walked partway
toward the van,
stopping a good
fifty feet away.

Without turning his eyes
away from that woman,
his lip curled back
to show his teeth,
Malsum backed up slowly
until he stood at Malian's side.

"Things are just fine,"
Malian said.

"I'm only staying
with my grandparents
until the shelter in place
orders are over.
My parents know where I am.
You can call them."

"In that case, I need,"
the woman said,
"to come inside."

Malian shook her head.
"No, you do not.
I'll give you their number.
You can call them up
whenever you want."

The woman opened her mouth
as if to say something more,
but stopped when Malsum
opened his mouth
and let out a long, deep growl.
Her eyes fixed

on the big dog,
the woman
took out her phone.
Then, as Malian recited
the number,
she keyed it in.

"Okay," Malian said,
putting on a big smile.
"Thanks so much
for your concern."
She held up her hand
and waved.
"Bye-bye now."

The woman did not
look very happy,
but she turned her car
back on, revved the engine,
and then, sending
a plume of gravel
into the air,
she drove away.

"All right, both of you!"
a voice said
from behind her.
It was her grandfather,
the carved bear
in his left hand.
He'd just come
out of the house.

"Wish we'd had
a dog like that
back when I was little.
Might've kept them
from taking me
away to that
dang Indian school."

Or my mom
to foster care,
Malian thought.

"You are such
a good friend," she said

as she and her
grandfather both
knelt down
and Malsum rolled over
onto his back
so they could stroke
his broad chest.

chapter eight

a moose story

When Malian walked back
into the house,
Grandma Frances motioned
for her to sit down.
She pushed the bowl of dried
moose meat over toward her.

"Have some of this, granddaughter.
It's good for what ails you."

Malian smiled.
That was what

her grandmother
always said
about whatever food
it was that she served.
It's good for what ails you.

"This is from the moose
that your great-uncle Philip
shot last year. It was a good
big one that decided
to give itself to him."

Her grandmother paused.
Malian said nothing,
knowing what
would be coming next.

"I ever tell you the moose story?"

Malian was pretty sure
she'd heard it before.

But no way was she
going to tell her grandma
that she'd already heard it.
Not only would that
have been rude,
it might've ended up
with her grandmother
not telling the story at all.

Plus, even when
she was told a story
she'd heard before,
there was always
something in that story
that was more.

Part of that might be
because every storyteller
had their own way
of seeing a story,
without really changing it.

Or maybe it was
because of what
her grandfather
often said—
that all the old stories
are so alive
that even when you hear
one of them again,
that story may decide
to show you
something new.

"I would really
like to hear that story,"
Malian said,
picking up a piece
of moose meat.

"Well," her grandmother said,
"there was this family of moose
all sitting in their lodge

around the fire and relaxing.
Then all of a sudden
what came floating in
through the door
of that lodge
was a pipe,
trailing smoke behind it.
None of those moose
reached out
at first for that pipe.
They knew what
it would mean
if they took it.
But then one of the young
bull moose said,
'I'll be the one
to take that pipe.'
He reached out for it
and as soon as he touched it,
he was no longer
in that lodge.

He was running
through the snow.
Behind him
was a man on snowshoes.
With those snowshoes on
he not only kept up
with that young moose,
he gained on it.
Then, when that hunter
got close enough
he stopped and
lifted up his gun.
Seeing that,
the young bull moose
turned to give the man
a good target.
Then the man fired.

"The next thing
that young moose knew,
he woke up

back in the lodge unharmed.
He looked around
at the other moose.
He said,
'You see, it's a good thing
to accept a gift like that.
Whenever a human
hunts that way,
it's good for us
to give ourselves.
That way
he only takes our meat
but does not harm our spirit.'"

Grandma Frances paused,
looked straight at Malian.
"And that is why,"
she said,
"we got this moose meat today.
Your uncle Philip
offered a gift of tobacco
as he asked that moose
to share its body with him."

"That is really good,"
Malian said.
"Is it okay
if I take a piece
out to Malsum?"

"Here,"
her grandma said,
"take two."

As Malian
walked outside,
she thought about
how hearing a story
told that way
made her feel good,
reminded her
they were still part
of something good,
something older
and longer lasting
than the moment
they were in.

They might be
forced for now
to stay home
because of the virus
but their spirits,
like that of the moose,
were still free to travel.
And the old connection
remained between them
and the natural world
always around them,
a world that could
give itself to you
if you just did
the right thing.

"Like sharing
this meat with you,"
Malian said
to Malsum,
who sat patiently
wagging his tail

as she held out

the first piece of

the moose meat to him.

chapter nine

potatoes

It was raining outside.
Malsum was nowhere
to be seen, but Malian
could feel his presence.
There was a place
he'd found, just under
the porch where he
went at night
and in weather like this.
There he could
still look out
and keep an eye on things
as their self-appointed protector.

The weather was still
not warm enough
to plant anything
in the small garden
her grandparents
kept out back.

But this rain would
be a good thing.
Even if it turned
into snow
that would still be good,
putting moisture
into the earth.

"This rain sure is cold,
just might turn to snow,"
Grampa Roy said.
"You know, nosis, grandchild,
early spring snow like this,
we call white manure.
Fertilizes the ground

where it falls.
Makes me wish
I'd already put in
some of my potatoes."

Malian watched
the cold raindrops
splashing down
on the black plastic
her grandparents used
to cover the mulch
on top of the garden,
the heat breaking it down
into good dark earth.
Cooking it real good
all through the winter,
was what Grampa Roy
had said.

"Potatoes," Grampa Roy said,
sort of half to himself.
"Always the first
to be planted up here.

You know potatoes
came from Andean folks,
up in the mountains
of South America
where it gets
a lot colder than this.
They had hundreds and
hundreds of kinds.
Problem in Ireland,
when they had that
potato famine
I mentioned
the other day.
Reason that all
their potatoes died
from the blight
was that they all
just grew one variety."

Ireland, Malian thought.
I used to dream
about going places
like Ireland and Spain.

But maybe now
the way the world was,
those were places
she would never go.
Then again, she thought
I've already traveled
more than most kids
on the reservation.
Some never even got
as far as the state capital
and she'd been to New York
and Boston and even,
that one summer, all the way
to Disney World in Florida.
Malian wished
the other kids on the rez
had the opportunities
she'd had.
And now,
through the stories
her grandparents
were sharing,
she was getting to travel

in another way,
feeling her spirit
travel through time,
being part of something
so much older,
so much deeper.

But still, here
in the physical world,
she could not leave
her grandparents' house.

And right now
she couldn't
even get online.

She looked again
at the screen of her iPad.
No bars were showing.

That meant
she could not
be part of lessons

her teacher had planned
for the day.
She wished that
their Internet connection
was better.
It was tough here
on the rez, getting
much of anything,
and the Internet
was no exception.

There had been a
new tower
about to be put in
not far from the rez
that would give
better service to
everybody here.
But work on that,
like work everywhere,
had just plain stopped
two months ago.
For some reason

the Internet
worked better at night—
that was how she was able
to link into Netflix
and watch things
with her grandparents.

Right now
what they were
mostly watching
were those old episodes
of Star Trek.

Her grandfather
put his hand
on her shoulder.
"Really coming down
out there, isn't it?"

Malian just nodded.
After spending
all this time with them,
she'd discovered

she didn't have
to say much at all.
Her grandparents
always seemed
to be able to know
what she was thinking.

"This here rain,"
Grampa Roy said,
"puts me in mind
of one of our old stories.
The one about
the good planter.
Want to hear it?"

This time,
she answered out loud.
"I would love to."

"Well," Grampa Roy said,
"there was this man
named Notkikad—
that means 'the planter'

in our language, you know.
No matter what happened,
whether rain or snow,
whether sunny or cold,
he always gave thanks
to the Creator.
And his crops were
some of the best.
But this one year
everything went wrong.
First there was frost,
killed everything he planted.
He planted again, but then
it got so hot,
everything dried up.
Then, when he put in
almost the last of his seeds,
big flocks of birds came in
and ate up everything.

"But there was still time.
for one last planting
and just enough seeds left.

They grew pretty good.
But then, wouldn't you know,
an early frost came
and everything
all shriveled up and died.

"Even so, though he figured
he and his family
might starve over the winter,
before he went to bed
he said a prayer
of thanks to the Creator.

"A cold wind was blowing
and there was snow in the air,
but that night as he slept
he had a good dream.
In that dream
he heard a voice
saying to him
I will give you a gift
of new seeds

and a special time
to plant them.

"When he woke up,
there at the foot of his bed
was a bag of seeds,
bigger seeds than any
he'd ever seen before.
He went outside.
It was sunny and warm
and the snow had melted away.
He planted those seeds
and just as soon
as he put them
into the ground
they started to pop up.
The sun kept shining
and it stayed warm
for the next seven days
as those plants kept growing.
By the end of that week
he saw that he'd have

more than enough
to feed his family
for the entire winter.
Just as soon as he finished
harvesting those crops,
the weather changed
and the snow came back in."

Grampa Roy chuckled.
"We don't have
any of those seeds now,
but our Creator
still gives us
that special time of year.
Nibun Alnoba,
a person's summer.
The white people call it
Indian summer."

As her grandfather
finished the story,
the rain had stopped.
Malian looked up.

In the sky to the west,
a rainbow had appeared.
"We call that
the coat worn by the rain,"
her grandfather said.
"I take it as a sign
that tomorrow I ought to
put in some potatoes."
From under the porch,
a loud woof came—
as if Malsum was agreeing.

Then Malian heard
a soft ding
from behind them.
She looked back into
the house.
There on the table
where she always worked
the face of her iPad
had lit up again.
She had two bars
and time enough

to get in
to the last half
of the day's lesson.

"I guess," Grampa Roy said,
"that device of yours
likes seeing a rainbow, too."

WOOF!
Malsum barked
in agreement.

chapter ten

pictures

Malian sat between
her grandparents
in the porch swing.
The big photo album
was in her lap.

Photo albums.

Every Native family
at Penacook had one.

It was a warm
late May day,
the first one over 70°
since the snow departed.
The three of them

sat looking
at the first picture
in the album.
It was of an old man
with a handlebar mustache.

"Just about every man
here in Penacook
had one of them 'staches
back then in the late 1800s,"
Grampa Roy said.
"They were the style then."
Then he chuckled.
"Sometimes I think men grew them
just so that they wouldn't look
like all the white people
thought us Indians oughta look.
Clean shaven and wearing
a headdress like Sitting Bull."

He shook his head.
"Or maybe it was also

because back when all of us men
were kids in the Indian school
we had our hair cut short
and had to dress in uniforms.
Growing a mustache that way
was kind of a statement.
That we were going to look
the way we wanted
and not the way
other folks wanted us to."

Her grandmother
gently rested
her hand on the page
where that photo was pasted.
"This man was your great-
great-grandfather," she said.
"He was a chief and an author, too."

Malian nodded.
She'd read his book.
It rested now back in its

special place as
the very first book
on the top shelf
of her grandmother's bookcase.

Her grandmother had copies
of every book written
about their people
and, in fact, just about
every book written
about any of the
Native American nations
of New England.
Most of them
were by white people.

"Which is why you want
to read their books,"
her grandmother had said.
"Not because they got it right,
but because you always
want to know what they
are thinking about us."

Grampa Roy had laughed
long and hard
when she said that.
"Did you know," he said,
"that all us Wabanakis
are anal-retentive,
whatever that means.
That's what one of them
ethnologists decided."

Malian ran her finger
along the crinkled edge
of the album's dark cover.

"Can we look again
at the pictures of you
and Grampa when you
were my age in school?"

Her grandmother
flipped the pages
to the photographs
of two children.

Their faces dead serious,
they stared at the camera.
The short-haired boy
who was her grampa
was dressed in a military uniform,
the girl who'd be
her grandmother wore
a long shapeless dress.

"These were the pictures
sent home to our parents,"
her grandmother said.
"That was the only way
they got to see us
because we were kept
at that school
month after month,
year after year."

Malian bit her lip
as she thought about that.
It was so hard for her
to be away from

her own parents now.
But she knew it was only
until things were safe
and they could talk
over the phone
and see each other's faces
on their screens.

Just that morning
she'd done FaceTime with them,
first her mother
and then her father,
holding the phone
and smiling up at her.

"I miss you both so much,"
she'd said, then
found it hard to talk.

"Are you okay?"
her mother asked.
Then, as she nodded
her head, forcing

a smile onto her face,
she'd managed to say
that things were good,
that she really loved
being with Grampa and Grandma.

"You're our warrior girl,"
her mother said.
Then her father,
who always seemed
to know what
she needed to hear,
spoke in his storytelling voice.

"Malian, do you know who
you remind us of right now?
The one in our old stories
who is called
the Woman Who Walks Alone.
She's the one who teaches
the birds new songs,
who makes a bed of moss
on the mountaintop

to watch the stars
swirl through the night
or sleeps with the bears
in their dens.
The one who needs
no man to tell her
what to do, although
when others need help,
she is always there."

They talked more
after that, but that story
was all she needed
to remember,
to remind her
just how lucky she was.

What would it be like
to not even see
your mother's smile
or hear the soft voice
of your father telling you
how proud he was

that you were taking
care of Grandma Frances
and Grampa Roy?
Just the thought
of that made her heart
want to break.

Her grandfather
ran his bent index finger
over the picture
of himself in the album.
"Can't really say
it was all bad.
Made some
of the best friends
I ever had in that school."

He lifted up
his finger and looked at it.
"Them nuns left me
some souvenirs.
Every knuckle on
both my hands

got broken one time
or another
from being hit
with that heavy ruler
Sister Anna Louise
always kept in her pocket."

Her grandmother started
flipping pages,
stopping when she came
to a picture Malian loved.
It was the first picture
ever taken of her father,
a chubby baby
being held up high
by both her grandparents.

"We called him
the miracle baby,"
Grandma Frances said.
"Last thing we expected
was to have another boy
after we both turned forty.

But he was a blessing
and your uncles and aunts
were like second parents,
all of them being
ten or more years older."

Grampa Roy let out
one of his deep chuckles.
"The only ones upset
were the Indian Health Service.
They'd thought for sure
they had made certain
your grandmother wouldn't
have any more children."

Malian found it hard
to understand
how people could do
something like that
to another person,
but she kept listening
to what her grandparents
thought she needed to know.

"Back then,"
Grandma Frances continued,
"when your father was born,
it was still common
for the Indian Health Service
to make it so that Indian women
could not give birth
to any more children
after they had had two or three.
Whenever a woman
went in to a free clinic,
they'd offer to do
a full health checkup.
And when she woke,
they would not tell her
what they'd done—
an operation
to prevent her from
ever having more kids."

Malian turned
another page
and then stopped.

It was hard to
believe what she
had just heard . . .
and what she saw.

"Looks just like him,
don't he?"
Grampa Roy said.

Malian nodded.
The picture with the year
1918 written on it
showed a man
in an old-fashioned
army uniform
with a dog by his side.

"That man there
is your great-great-grampa
Arthur Bowman.
Picture was taken
right here at Penacook
before he went overseas.

He called his dog Wolf.
Wolf just disappeared
and was nowhere to be seen
after Arthur got on the train."

"You know,"
her grandmother added,
"funny thing
is that while
he was in France
he had another dog
that just showed up
and got adopted
by his unit.
Looked
so much like his,
he called it Wolf Two.
Stayed by his side
until the day before
the war ended and he
was to be shipped back home.
Wolf Two was just gone
that very next day.

But when Arthur
got back to Penacook,
can you guess
who was waiting
by his front door?"

Malsum had been sitting
out by the mailbox.
But as soon
as Grandma Frances
stopped talking,
the big dog
came trotting over.
One big leap
brought him up
onto the porch.
He put his front paws
on Malian's knees,
leaned in close,
and stared at the picture
of her great-great-grandfather
and the dog named Wolf
for a long minute

before turning to rest
his chin in her lap.

Grampa Roy reached over
to scratch behind
the big dog's ears.
"Some of the most loyal
folks I've ever known
have been dogs," he said.
"They always
find some way to
come back home."

chapter eleven

sergeant ed

"Hello, the house?"
a voice called
from outside.

Malian, who had
been trying
to figure out
what to do about
the assignment
she'd just been given
to write an essay
for her teacher,
welcomed
the interruption
because she was feeling

totally stuck
about finding a topic.

She opened the door
and looked out.

A tall man
wearing a mask
was standing
next to the mailbox.

Despite the mask,
Malian knew
just who he was.

There was only
one person at Penacook
who was six ten and
drove a tribal police car.
It had to be Sergeant Ed.

Despite the mask,
Malian knew

there was a smile
on the broad face of
the former Indian league
star center.
Sergeant Ed
was always smiling
and everyone
on the rez
liked him.

It seemed that
everyone included dogs.
To Malian's surprise,
Malsum was sitting
next to the tall tribal cop
and letting him
scratch his neck.

Sergeant Ed straightened
and held up his cell phone.

"Call me," he said

in a loud voice.
"You got me
on your contacts, right?
Been trying
to reach you today."

Malian looked at her phone.
Three missed calls.
She'd forgotten
to turn the ringer back on.

She hit the number
to reply.

"Hey!" the voice
of Sergeant Ed said
in phony surprise.
"Who is this?"

Malian laughed.
She could see why
people loved the way

Sergeant Ed deployed
his sense of humor first
in just about
any situation.

"We're fine," she said.
"Is anything wrong?"

Sergeant Ed grinned.
"Just checking up on
a report about some fierce dog
been hanging around here.
Apparently, not this one."
He reached down and
scratched behind Malsum's ears.
"You're a real teddy bear,
aren't you, boy?"

Malsum dropped down
and rolled over
onto his back,

prompting the sergeant
to lower himself
to one knee to rub
the big dog's chest.

"Got this complaint from
the state health service lady.
Which is not unusual.
She's always complaining
about us Penacooks."
Sergeant Ed shrugged
as he continued to run
his hands over Malsum's belly.
"So where did you
get this guy from?"

"He just sort of
showed up," Malian said

Sergeant Ed nodded.
"You know," he said,

"them two white spots
over his eyes make him
what in the old days we
called a four-eyed dog,
sort of a medicine animal."
Malian smiled
but didn't tell
the sergeant she'd already
heard about a dog
like that from
her grandfather.

"My great-grandma,"
the sergeant continued,
"tole me a story
about a dog like that.
Wish I could remember it.
But you know, I bet
your grandmother remembers.
She is one of the best
storytellers around here.

As well as about the best
frybread maker—next to
my aunt Gertrude, of course.
You ought to ask her
'bout that four-eyed dog story."

"I will," Malian replied.

"Okay then,"
Sergeant Ed said.
"Seeing as how everything
is all good here,
I guess my job is done.
You have a real good day.
And you and my friend here,
you both take care
of your grandparents."

The tall sergeant climbed
into his police car
and leaned out the window.

"If that real fierce dog
ever shows up here again,
you gimme a call, okay?"

"Okay," Malian agreed,
trying not to laugh.

"Good, now
I got to skedaddle.
Left Stanley alone
on the roadblock.
Want to make sure
he's not getting
any more trouble
from the staties.
Trying to tell us
we cannot stop
and turn back
every single car
that's not from here
trying to take the shortcut
through our reservation.

I just told them
state patrolmen
Oh yes, we can,
'specially with
this pandemic.
Then I just
grinned down at them
and made 'em wait
till we got our
tribal lawyer there."
Sergeant Ed chuckled.
"Who pointed out
it's there in the treaty
we got the right
to enforce traffic
on any road
goes through
our reservation."

As Sergeant Ed drove away
Malsum rolled over,
sat up, turned,

and looked at Malian,
his mouth open
in a wide doggy grin.

"My golly," Malian said.
"you are one smart dog,
aren't you?"

Malsum nodded his head.

chapter twelve

been there

The weather had finally broken.
The sun was shining down
like a smiling face.
Malian and Grampa Roy
were spading up the garden
behind the house.

They'd both been
watching on her iPad
a story on the
CNN newsfeed
about the protests
going on around the country,
people standing up
for racial justice.

"About time,"
her grandfather had said.
"Let's keep those folks
in our thoughts.
Seems to me right now,
that's the best
we can do,
seeing as how
we can't be with them."
Then he'd stood up.
"And seeing as how
the garden won't
spade up itself,
seems to me
like it's time
to go outside.
Ready to go?"

"You bet,"
she'd replied.

Malsum was sitting
at the garden edge

close to where
Malian was working.

When they'd started spading,
he'd come over to them
and begun to dig
with his front paws.

"Go for it, boy,"
Grampa Roy had said.
"Save us the trouble."
But all Malsum did
was make a shallow hole
where he could sit
in the cool earth,
settle back, and watch.

Grandma Frances
was inside making pies
using some of the rhubarb
they'd just picked
from the patch
to the side of the garden.

Within a few days,
they would also be
harvesting asparagus
from the bed
her grandfather had made
more than fifty years ago.
Small white spears were
starting to poke up
from the ground
rich with mulch.

Her grandparents' garden
was not a big one.
Only thirty feet long
and twelve feet wide.
But more than big enough
to grow all the corn
and beans and squash
they would need.
Plus they had lettuce
and radishes already planted
at the edge of the garden

when it was still
not yet warm enough
for most other things.
And on the other side
of the garden
in a separate bed
her grandfather
had finally put in
his beloved potatoes.

"If we could still
go out like we did
in the old days,
gathering medicine
from the woods
and fish from the streams,
there'd be no need
to go to any grocery store,"
Grandma Frances always said.

Her grandfather stopped
and looked over at her

and the big dog.
"Sure a lot to be thankful
for today, innit?" he said.

Malsum woofed
his agreement as
Malian nodded.

"I guess you could say
we're a lot like Notkikad,"
she said, bringing a smile
to her grandfather's face.

"You know," he said,
"seems like you remember
stories as well as
your father always did."

Malian shook her head.
"I don't know," she said.
"I just wish I could find
one that would fit in
with the assignment

I have to do now.
The new one for
my language arts course."

"What sort of story
are you looking for?"

"Well," she said,
"we're supposed to write
something that has to do
with everything that's
going on right now.
But I'm not even
sure where to start.
Nothing like this has
ever happened before."

Grampa Roy
shook his head.
"That's what some
might say. But not us.
In a way, we've been
through all this before."

Malian put down
her spading fork.
She sat on one
of the cedar stumps
her grandfather had placed
around the garden
to use as stools
or tables or whatever
they might be handy for.
The best way to ask for
a story was just
to be ready and listen.

Her grandfather sat down
on the stump next to hers.
"They ever talk in
your school about
how many people
were here before Columbus?"

Malian nodded.
"Most of the books say
maybe two or three million."

Grampa Roy nodded back.
"Yep, that's what they say."
He paused, took out
his big red handkerchief,
and wiped his brow.
"But I've done a lot
of reading and research
over the years and I've listened
to what the elders told.
And I'd say that just here
in what they called
the United States
there were at least
twenty times that many.

"When those new people came
they brought with them
all kinds of germs.
Measles, whooping cough,
influenza, smallpox, all sorts
of diseases that we never
had any names for.
By the time those Pilgrims

landed on the coast
to the east of here,
all that they found
was empty land because
our people there had died
or run to get away
from all that sickness."

Grampa Roy
shook his head,
then he grinned.
"Maybe what
you ought to write
is just *Been There, Done That*."

chapter thirteen

the assignment

It was a week after
Malian had told
her eighth-grade teacher
the things her grandparents
had shared with her
about how the Indian Health Service
had made it so
Indian women
could not have
any more children.

Ms. Mendelson had not
believed her at first—
until the two of them
did an Internet search.

"I am so sorry,"
Ms. Mendelson had said.
It had made
the two of them closer.
Especially when Malian
pointed out to her
what she'd just found
on the Internet
about something called
the Eugenics Project
in the nearby
state of Vermont.
It had been set up
to sterilize
what they called
"unfit" people,
a lot of them
Native men and women,
back in the 1930s.

The scientists
of Nazi Germany
had based some

of their ideas on what
was done in Vermont.

That was when
Ms. Mendelson
shared with Malian
that her own Jewish grandmother
was a Holocaust survivor
who'd been in
a concentration camp.

Malian thought about that
as she clicked on the link
to the class Zoom meeting,
thought about the way
so many things
tied in to each other.

Her face blurring
from the poor connection,
Ms. Mendelson
appeared on the screen.
"I know what your final assignment

is going to be," she said,
"I've been thinking a lot about everything
that is happening in the world now.
Some of the things you've
all shared with me in our
conversations, or handed in,
like Malian's short essay that reminded us
how Native American people
were so affected by other diseases
long before this pandemic,
made me start thinking differently.

"Then . . ." She paused,
her face looking troubled.
"I remembered something that happened to me.
It's made me realize that we need
to hear more of each other's stories."

Malian could tell
something was really bothering her.
"I am going to start by telling you
a story of my own. It won't be long,

but it will tell you something about me,
something I did not realize,
something I now need to share.

"It's about something that happened.
It happened before the virus came,
before the protests, before everything
that's so confusing today."

She paused, took a breath,
and then went on.

"I've never shared this story before,
not with anyone, but now is the time.
As you all know, I used to take
the city bus from my home to school.
Even though it was a cold day
and everyone was all bundled up,
it was sunny and beautiful and so
I got off two blocks early
to walk across the park
but as I started walking

I got this feeling
that someone was following me.
I looked back quickly and I could see
a tall figure wearing a hoodie.
He was too far away
to make out his features,
but I guessed he was Black.

"I started to walk faster then
and so did he, catching up on me.
No one else was around.
I felt so afraid.
I reached into my pocket,
just in case I had to dial 911.
But when I couldn't find my phone,
I panicked and I started to run.
Behind me that person
began to run too!

"That was when I slipped and fell down.
I stayed on the ground, unable to move.

I thought for sure I was going to be hurt.
But then I heard a familiar voice.
'Teacher? Ms. Mendelson, are you okay?'
When I looked up I saw a hand
holding out my cell phone to me.
'Here, you dropped this on the bus.'

"It was one of my students
from two years ago,
a boy who's in
high school now.
He helped me up
and I said thank you.
But I never told him
how afraid I'd been.
I never told him what
it taught me that day.
Even though I thought
I wasn't racist,
something in me
was still afraid

of people with skin color
different from mine."
Ms. Mendelson's face
on Malian's iPad disappeared
as the connection faltered.
Only a second passed, but when
the image resolved itself again,
her teacher's eyes looked wet.

"I never apologized to Rodney,
for what I was thinking,"
Ms. Mendelson said.
"But now I'm apologizing
to all of you for not
being a better teacher."

She paused again, took a sip of water
from the bottle on top of her desk.
"I think that what we all need now
is to know each other better.
That's why I'm asking you to share
whatever it is you want us to know
about you and your family.

"You can tell your story
however you want.
Long or just a few paragraphs.
Read it aloud, put it up on the screen,
play music behind it, that's all fine.
If you'd like, include some images,
even make a movie if you want.
That all would be fine. It's up to you.
But let's use this chance
to get to know each other better.
That way, maybe something good
can come out of this hard year.
That is what I hope."

Ms. Mendelson swallowed hard.
"Is this assignment clear enough?
Is it something you'd all like to do?
Send me a yes, a thumbs-up, or whatever
to let me know how you feel."

Right away, the messages began coming
one after another in the chat box.
Yeses, thumbs-up, hearts, and even

a few emojis of smiling faces.
When the final one came up,
Ms. Mendelson nodded her head.

"Okay," she said, "we're all agreed.
Now, in case anyone hasn't noticed,
with all of our days being the same,
today is Friday." She smiled at her joke.
"So, this is your weekend assignment.
Next Monday, bright and early at ten,
we can start hearing from everyone.
Meanwhile, take care of yourselves
and please be kind to each other."
She lifted her hand to touch
her screen and then was gone.

A voice spoke from over
Malian's shoulder.

"Want your grandma and me to help
some with that assignment of yours?"

Malian spun her chair around
and wrapped her arms
around her grandfather.

"More than anything."

chapter fourteen

malian's story

Malian had asked
to be the last one
to do her presentation.

"Are you sure
you won't be nervous?"
her teacher had asked.

"No," she'd said.
"Waiting is something
you get used to
when you're Native American."

Her teacher had started
to laugh, then caught herself.

"I'm sorry," she said.
"I don't mean to
make light of your
people's history."

"It's okay to laugh,"
Malian said.
"That was a joke . . .
sort of."

Of the twenty kids
in her class only fifteen
were able to get online
for their presentation.
Each one was just
ten minutes long
with a two-minute
break in between.

Malian was glad she was last;
it made it easier for her
to really listen to what

each of her classmates
had to share.

She found herself
learning things about them
she'd never known before.
Some had families
that had been in Boston
for generations—though
none of the others
were Native Americans.
But no one had a genealogy
longer than Francine Woo.
Her family had moved
to the city from San Francisco
five years ago.
She told the story of how
her father made a trip
to the archives in Beijing
to look up their family history.
"Can you guess how far
he was able to trace it back?"

she asked everyone.
"Two thousand and ten years.
But," she said, "the records
only listed the male heads
of the families and what scores
they had on their examinations."
Then she told the story
about her ancestor
who was a famous admiral.
He had sailed his ships
all around the world
and came to North America
years before Columbus.

Finally it was Malian's turn.
She'd thought a lot about
what she was going to say.
There were so many things
her teacher and classmates
did not know.
But the question was,
which things should she share?

She didn't want
to make people feel bad.
But she also wanted to be honest.

Should she tell them about
the time two centuries ago
when the colonial government
offered bounties for Indian scalps?

She had decided not
to tell that story.
It would be too hard
for them to take.

She took a deep breath
and began to talk.
She told them how
her own mother was taken
from her family
and adopted out.

She told them about
the boarding schools,

where her grandparents
were forbidden to speak
their language and were told
to be ashamed of their own culture.

"Those were the old days,
not the good old days," she said.
And then she smiled.
"No one should feel guilty
about the past. Unless
they're not doing
anything about the present.
That's what
my grandparents say.
Think about what we
are doing now and how
it will affect the world
seven generations from today,
and not just in the next election."

As she spoke, she heard Malsum
walk up behind her, his nails
clacking on the floor.

It was the first time
he'd ever come into the house.
"We have to think,"
my grandparents say,
"about every living thing,
about all of our relations."

As she spoke those words,
behind her the big dog
stood up on his hind legs
and gently put his front paws
on Malian's shoulders.

She put her right hand
on Malsum's big paw.
"My friend and I," she said,
"want to tell you this story.

"Long ago the Creator decided
it was time to make human beings.
The Creator wanted them to be strong
and so they were made out of stone.
They were strong for sure.

But because their hearts were hard,
they crushed everything
with their heavy feet.
All they cared about was themselves.
So the Creator took those first people,
broke them up into stones,
and put them back on the land.
That is why there are so many
stones here in our land.
Then the Creator looked around
and saw the ash trees, rooted deep
in the land and dancing in the wind,
joining their branches together
with the other trees around them.
So the next human beings
were made from the ash trees,
and like those ash trees,
they were rooted in the ground
and their hearts were always growing.
Those trees were my ancestors."

Malian paused;
it seemed as if

she could feel everyone
listening to her.

"My grandparents say
that is what we must do now.
Take care of each other
and take care of our land.
We need to be kind to each other
and to all living things,
make the circle strong
for those who come after us.
Instead of just standing up alone
like those first stone people,
we need to bend our knees
and touch the earth."

She heard one of the
kids who were listening.
"Look at them . . . her grandparents."
"Even the dog!" another kid said.

Malian looked back
over her shoulder.

Behind her, in full
view of the camera,
her grandparents had each
knelt down on one knee.
Malsum was now sitting
in between her grandparents
with one front leg bent
as if he too was kneeling.

Malian felt tears forming in her eyes.
"I am going to end it here,"
she managed to say.
"I'm going to do it in our old way.
Instead of saying
goodbye in English,
I'm going to leave you
with these words from our
old Wabanaki language.
Wlipamkaani, nidobak.
Have a good journey, my friends."

chapter fifteen

afterward

School had been out
for three weeks.
Summer had come
to the rez.
Malian sat
on her grandparents' porch,
smelling the lilacs
that bloomed by the walk.
Even though
it was too warm
for him to place
his head in her lap,
Malsum was there,
right next to her.

Malian smiled
as she thought
of all the things
that had happened
since she'd found herself
unable to leave
her grandparents.

She felt good
about the way
she'd been able
to help them.
And, not only that,
she felt even
more sure about
being at Penacook.
"I'm just like you,"
she said to Malsum
as she leaned over
to stroke his head.
"I know this place
is our home."

She looked down
the poorly paved road.
No sign yet of their car.
Now that things
seemed to have let up some,
people were traveling,
at least a little,
and the reservation
was no longer
locked down.
Her parents were coming
to pick her up.
She'd be back home
and that made her glad.

But, even so,
she also wished
she could somehow be
both places at once.
Or maybe have one
of those transporters
like those in the

Star Trek shows
her grampa loved.

"But you can come with me,"
she whispered to Malsum.
"Mom and Dad told me
they'd love to have you
as their honored guest."

The big dog
pricked up his ears.
He lifted his head
and looked down the road.
Then he stood up
and looked straight
into Malian's eyes.
"Oh," she said. "Oh."

Malsum nodded,
turned, and began to run.
He disappeared into
the small woods

behind the house
just as Malian
heard the crunching
of tires approaching
on the broken road.

"His place is here,"
a soft voice said
from behind her.
Malian turned to look.
Her grandmother
was in the doorway
and her grandfather
came up next to her.

"Don't worry,"
her grandfather said,
"a rez dog knows
where it needs to be.
He'll be here
for you for sure
when you come back again."
"After all,"

her grandmother said
as Malian stood
and wrapped her arms
around both of them,
"just like us
you're a rez dog too."